SEP 02

LATINOS IN THE LIMELIGHT

Christina Aguilera

Antonio Banderas

Jeff Bezos

Oscar De La Hoya

Cameron Díaz

Scott Gomez

Salma Hayek

Enrique Iglesias

John Leguizamo

Jennifer Lopez

Ricky Martin

Pedro Martínez

Freddie Prinze Jr.

Selena

Carlos Santana

Sammy Sosa

CHELSEA HOUSE PUBLISHERS

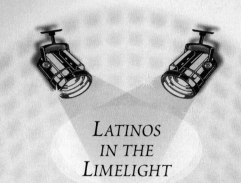

LATINOS
IN THE
LIMELIGHT

Enrique Iglesias

Cathy Alter Zymet

CHELSEA HOUSE PUBLISHERS
Philadelphia

Frontis: Since winning a Grammy in 1997 for his album *Vivir,* Enrique Iglesias has become a world-famous celebrity.

CHELSEA HOUSE PUBLISHERS

Editor in Chief: Sally Cheney
Director of Production: Kim Shinners
Production Manager: Pamela Loos
Art Director: Sara Davis
Editor: Bill Conn
Production Editor: Diann Grasse

Layout by
21st Century Publishing and Communications, Inc.
http://www.21cpc.com

The Chelsea House World Wide Web address is
http://www.chelseahouse.com

First Printing

1 3 5 7 9 8 6 4 2

CIP applied for ISBN 0-7910-6478-6

CONTENTS

MAKING

HIS-STORY

For three years, the "Divas" reigned. Starting in 1998, music video channel VH1 began broadcasting all-star revues showcasing the hottest female singers in the recording industry.

First came Celine Dion, Aretha Franklin, Mariah Carey, Gloria Estefan, and Shania Twain. The "Divas" special ranked as the most-watched single broadcast in VH1 history. The next year showcased Tina Turner, Cher, Whitney Houston, and Brandy for the reprise, "VH1 Divas Live '99." That show topped its predecessor in the ratings.

But enough was enough. Days after the "VH1 Divas 2000: A Tribute to Diana Ross," the music channel decided it was time to inject a little testosterone into the mix.

Five mega-star male performers spanning several generations and musical styles would appear together on stage in "Men Strike Back."

"It was our guess that the audience was more than ready for some very sexy men," said Wayne Isaak, VH1's executive vice president of talent and music programming and creator of the "Divas" specials.

When a wave of Latin music swept across the U.S. in the 1990s, Iglesias was at the forefront with hits like "Bailamos." With his good looks and natural sense of style, Iglesias was an immediate success with audiences young and old.

Enter Enrique Iglesias. A relative newcomer, Enrique was selected on a bill showcasing Sting, Backstreet Boys, Tom Jones, D'Angelo, and Sisqo. The only female singer permitted in this exclusive Boys' Club was Christina Aguilera, a bona fide mini-diva who shimmied her way into the line up.

By the end of the two-hour concert, taped at New York's famous Madison Square Garden, Enrique had gained the respect of his male colleagues, won over an audience of millions, and caught the eye of the girl, Christina Aguilera.

Sting set the tone, walking on stage clad in a simple black sweater and delivering a spare, haunting rendition of "Roxanne," accompanied only by his guitar and saxophonist Branford Marsalis. As the singer launched into another Police classic, "Don't Stand So Close To Me," he was joined by the Backstreet Boys, who provided some silky harmonies.

By now, the audience was warmed up and raring to go. The air in the Garden was charged with excitement. When Enrique strode on stage in an impeccably tailored dark-gray shirt and matching pants, the audience squealed in delight. Enrique's diehard fans knew that he had been on the scene since 1995, with the release of his self-titled debut. But many in the audience, which included celebrities such as Jenna Elfman, Matthew McConaughey, and Susan Sarandon, had never set eyes on this six-foot-two-inch Spanish-born hunk.

It didn't take long for everyone to fall under Enrique's spell. When Enrique began to belt out his hit song "Bailamos," which loosely translates into "We're Dancing," the crowd followed his lead. They jumped to their feet, stomping and clapping to the music. His

Two generations of high-powered vocal talent met on VH1's Men Strike Back when 1960s hit-maker Tom Jones joined Iglesias on stage to sing Bruce Springsteen's song "Fire."

performance seemed to say, "Come on! Let's leave all our inhibitions at the door and just have a good time!"

By the time Tom Jones joined him for a hot version of Bruce Springsteen's "Fire," it was clear that Enrique had turned up the heat on his own celebrity status. Although he was reportedly suffering from a sore throat, Enrique sang with force and passion. His combination of high energy, sensual ballads, and good looks were the right ingredients for superstardom.

Despite suffering from a sore throat, Enrique delivered a passionate performance at VH1's showcase of male singing stars, a response to three years of "Diva" specials featuring women singers.

Enrique seemed bent on confirming to himself and to the public that he was more than just a flash in the pan. He hadn't let up since "Bailamos" had reached Number One on the *Billboard Hot 100* and helped catapult the *Wild Wild West* soundtrack into the double-platinum stratosphere.

And Enrique didn't discourage the fervor his high energy and his reputation as a heartthrob create. Asked by a People magazine reporter about the problem of female fans who rush the stage during concerts, he replied: "I can't stop performing, I have to keep going. If it was one of my favorite singers, I would do the exact same thing."

Enrique, with his desire to please his fans, was destined for a place in the heartthrob Hall of Fame. When he joined the rest of the all-star lineup for a version of Sting's "Every Breath You Take," it was clear that Enrique already had one special admirer sharing the stage with him: Christina Aguilera.

The pair had met a few months earlier, when they sang a duet during the Super Bowl halftime show. Ever since, Christina had made no secret of her attraction to Enrique. As soon as every last "Breath" was taken, she made a beeline across the stage and gave Enrique a big hug. Later that night, they were together at the "Men Strike Back" after-party and at 2:00 A.M., they showed up at Nell's, a hot Manhattan night-spot. There, Christina and Enrique performed a steamy dance together that lasted for about twenty minutes.

To the night crawlers at Nell's, and indeed, to the rest of the world, it seemed like Enrique Iglesias had it all: a hit song, a starring gig on VH1, and a beautiful blond "Genie in a Bottle."

Enrique's life hasn't always been so charmed. In fact, his path has been filled with many bumps and obstacles—some set up by Enrique himself.

From the beginning, Enrique thrived on overcoming the odds, whether it was his immense shyness, or escaping from the hulking shadow of the fame of his father Julio Iglesias.

Just how did he turn his dreams into reality? The path that Enrique traveled to fame and success was quite an interesting journey.

At the Men Strike Back special, singer Christina Aguilera made no secret of her attraction to Enrique. Later, at a Manhattan nightspot, Christina and Enrique performed a steamy dance together.

2

FATHER'S DAY

E nrique almost always begins his interviews by making a simple request: "Please do not introduce me as the son of Julio Iglesias."

Few things bother Enrique Iglesias as much as the mention of his famous father, an internationally acclaimed Spanish crooner. Even as a small boy, Enrique wanted to be seen as his own person, with his own talents. He often walked away from any friend who exposed him as Julio Iglesias's son.

Still, it's hard *not* to think about Enrique without first considering Julio. To understand a son's hopes and dreams, as well as his frailties and fears, it is necessary to examine his father.

Enrique's story begins with the birth of his father, Julio Jose Iglesias, on September 23, 1943. Julio's father, Julio Iglesias Puga, was one of Madrid's leading gynecologists whose thriving career made it possible for the family to live in the wealthiest part of town. His mother, Rosario de la Cueva, often brought little Julio out onto one of the home's spacious wrought-iron balconies, where they sat and drank in the sights and sounds of the busy street below. A baby brother, Carlos, joined them eighteen months later.

Coupled with his vocal talent, Enrique's good looks rocketed him to heartthrob status among younger audiences.

For all their material riches, the Iglesias family lacked emotional wealth. From the time he was small, Julio was conscious of the cracks in his parents' marriage. He overheard rumors of his father's infidelities. Because of his unconditional love for his father, Julio sank into denial, and began to rationalize his father's unfaithfulness.

To the outside world, the family appeared to function like any other happy household. Rosario seemed to be a loving mother and dutiful wife. On the inside, she was a woman scorned. She boiled with anger. When her fury took over, the loyalties of her children were divided. Carlos stuck by his mother, and Julio formed a loyal attachment to his father.

The patterns carried into adulthood. Like his father, Julio would not remain loyal to one woman. He became known as a "Latin lover," while his brother Carlos remained with the same woman for many years. Ironically, as a young man, Julio was not considered very good looking and felt insecure in comparison to Carlos, considered by far the more handsome of the brothers.

"Julio had quite an inferiority complex about his looks compared to Carlos," reveals an old family friend. "Carlos was an exceptionally beautiful child with thick dark hair and beautiful long eyelashes. I think Julio got sick of people saying how lovely his brother was."

Because Julio had to rely on something other than his looks to get by, he cultivated a winning personality. He developed a social grace that would serve him well later on in his performing career.

Julio also became a champion soccer player. At fifteen, he was such a skilled goalkeeper that

Enrique was the child of a stormy marriage between Latin singer Julio Iglesias and Filipino beauty Isabel Preysler. The marriage ended while Enrique was still a boy. While Enrique continued to live with his mother in Madrid, he, along with his brother and sister, spent summers with their father in Miami.

he tried out for Real Madrid, Spain's premier professional soccer team. By the time he was twenty, Julio was on his way to becoming one of the most gifted athletes on the team, and he was earning a law degree at the Colegio Mayor de San Pablo.

But on the night of September 22, 1963, something happened that would change his life.

While on a college break, Julio and two of his schoolmates drove to Majadahonda, home to one of the biggest annual fiestas in Spain. Caught up in the party atmosphere, Julio danced in the town's square, ate dinner under the stars, whistled at the pretty girls, and lost every ounce of his inhibition—as well as his judgment.

Happy and carefree, Julio and his buddies

hopped into his car and sped off to another party, taking bends and curves at 100 mph. While making a tight hairpin turn, Julio's car spun violently out of control, teetered over a sharp precipice, and plunged to the ground below.

When he regained consciousness, Julio checked his friends and then himself for injuries. Amazingly, aside from a few cuts and scratches, everyone emerged from the accident remarkably intact—at least for the time being.

A month after the wreck, Julio began to notice a slight pain in his spine. He continued to play soccer, but before long, the pain was so bad that he could no longer perform routine blocks and kicks. In fact, he could barely stand up straight.

Forced to give up the game, Julio underwent a painful procedure to help identify the source of his pain. According to Julio's father, "A soft cyst had been growing on Julio's spine and causing gradual paralysis by compressing the vertebrae and the nerves."

Paralyzed from the waist down, Julio spent more than two weeks in the hospital, receiving treatments and round-the-clock care. When he was released, Julio went home in a wheelchair. Flat on his back and despondent, Julio harnessed his skill as an athlete to battle his toughest opponent: his paralysis.

Determined to walk again, he spent hours and hours a day willing his body to move. His "mind-over-matter" regimen, coupled with grueling rounds of physical therapy, eventually showed results. By 1966, he had gained enough control to move around using a cane. It took another two years before he could walk unassisted. Today, Julio's slight limp reminds him of the painful ordeal.

As soon as Julio began walking, he was eager to make up for lost time. He moved to England, where he brushed up on his English at Cambridge's Bell Language School. There, he met fellow Spaniard Enrique Bassat, who soon became his best friend (and namesake of his son).

Enrique convinced Julio that, if they were to stay in England, they'd need a plan for making money. Julio told Enrique he could sing a little, and his buddy immediately booked him a gig at the Airport Pub.

When Julio heard the wild applause of the audience, he was transported back to the soccer field. The attention was so irresistible that Julio became enamored with performing. He also was smitten with a beautiful young woman named Gwendoline Bollore. Encouraged by her love, Julio recorded "La Vida Sigue Igual" (Life Continues Just the Same).

That became the first hit single in a long list of achievements. In the ten years to follow, Julio performed 200 shows a year and sold more than 100 million albums worldwide. He also broke many hearts, including Gwendoline's, who could never compete with Julio's love of the spotlight.

The next woman to come between Julio and the stage was Isabel Preysler, a Filipino beauty whom Julio married in 1971. The entertainer entered the marriage with visions of happily ever after. Julio pledged to be true to his wife, but it didn't take long before he was repeating the same kinds of mistakes his father had made. When the couple's first daughter, Chabeli, was born on September 3,

Enrique's father, Julio Iglesias, achieved fame as a romantic singer in the 1970s. Enrique, however, was never content to live in his famous father's shadow and has worked hard to make a name of his own. Enrique begins most interviews with a simple request: "Please do not introduce me as the son of Julio Iglesias."

1971, Julio began a pattern of absence and adultery that eventually ruined the marriage.

He was even late for the delivery of his first child. "Well, he was working, he was on tour, which was the way it always was," explained Isabel, seeming to accept her fate.

For a few years, Isabel stayed busy caring for her baby daughter and son, Julio Jose, who was born on April 23, 1973, and was unaware of Julio's infidelities. But about the time Enrique was born, on May 8, 1975, Isabel had to face the fact that her marriage to Julio was in trouble.

Enrique's arrival into the world was the beginning of the end of Isabel and Julio's wedded bliss. Although he didn't understand the impact until much later in life, Enrique's early years of loss and abandonment helped shape the person he was destined to become.

ENRIQUE ALONE

In 1977, Julio Iglesias was at the pinnacle of his musical career. Unfortunately, he was at the peak of his womanizing career as well. Having been tipped off by a friend about Julio's latest indiscretion, Isabel confronted her husband.

"He didn't deny any of it, which was rather devastating," Isabel recalled. "He simply said, 'But you know you were the only one that mattered, you were the only one that I ever really loved.'"

Unwilling to live with his betrayals any longer, Isabel separated from Julio in 1978, and they announced that they were divorcing.

Enrique was three years old at the time his parents split. He had already grown accustomed to Julio's busy touring schedule and long absences from home. He was not, however, used to seeing his mother's great unhappiness. Enrique felt the impact of his parents' separation long into his adulthood.

The absence of a father figure created a void that nothing could fill. Enrique's loss was made more difficult when, the following year, Julio announced that he was moving to Miami, Florida. Julio saw his divorce as a good time to start over and a golden opportunity to break into the American music scene.

Enrique shows his sensitive side in a publicity photo.

Julio started building a huge estate called Indian Creek. Set in the lush, tropical gardens of Miami's most exclusive neighborhood, it had everything from indoor *and* outdoor pools to a forest of coconut trees framing the perimeter. Because Enrique, Carlos, and Chabeli would spend summers with him, Julio put every effort into making Indian Creek the perfect home-away-from-home for his children.

Enrique and his brother and sister always looked forward to visiting the compound. Although their father was frequently away on tour, the kids loved exploring their new home, playing on the tennis courts, and having great freedom to do whatever they wanted.

The siblings also loved their father's new girlfriend, Virginia Sipl. Without children of her own, and lonely from Julio's constant touring, Virginia embraced the Iglesias children. Enrique especially responded to her warmth and loving attention. In later interviews, he said he was never as content as when he was in Virginia's presence.

From 1978 until 1981, life for Enrique was uneventful. He split his time between Madrid and Miami, and found it easy to make friends wherever he was. His mother, now remarried and working as a successful journalist, took pride in watching her son's newfound ease with the world.

Things were going well until December 20, 1981, when Enrique's grandfather, Julio's father, was kidnapped and held for ransom in Spain.

"Nobody spoke a word to me," remembers Dr. Iglesias, who was sixty-six at the time of his kidnapping. "They would put food in front of me, and that was all, but they never communicated or answered my questions."

When Isabel called her ex-husband, terror seized Julio, and he was wracked with guilt. As one of the most popular entertainers of the day, Julio thought his celebrity made his family prime targets for foul play.

A rescue operation found Dr. Iglesias two days after his disappearance, but the experience changed the Iglesias family. Isabel and Julio became intensely protective of their children. Fearing for their lives, Isabel decided to send Enrique and his siblings to live with their father in Miami. With Julio's top-of-the-line security system and round-the-clock bodyguards, she knew her children would be safe and protected.

At first, Enrique was excited about the move. He associated Miami with warmth, comfort, and Virginia Sipl. But Enrique returned to an empty house. Virginia, tired of hearing about Julio's affairs, had broken up with him and moved out. And with Julio's work schedule keeping him away so often, Enrique and his brother and sister were often alone.

"Leaving my mother, it was very hard," Enrique confessed. "And having to start a new life, new friends, new school, different language. It wasn't easy."

Although Enrique spoke to his parents frequently by phone, he only saw his father once a month and his mother twice a year. Enrique's sense of isolation grew. He expressed his loneliness by acting up in elementary school, and was suspended in third grade for putting a lizard on his teacher's back.

Julio's manager, Alfredo Fraile, saw that Enrique was unhappy in his new home, and made every effort to invite the Iglesias children into his own household. Playing with the

Fraile children and watching their mother cook dinner, Enrique began to see what a happy family was like.

Alfredo says, "They saw life at our house—a wife, a husband, and children—was stable and normal and they were attracted to that because it was not their experience and it was what they wanted so much."

Alfredo became a father figure, and Enrique soon found a surrogate mother in his nanny, Elvira Olivares. She represented the affection and acceptance that was missing from his life. Despite having all the material things he could ever want—a lavish house, yachts, and expensive vacations—Enrique most wanted to be loved.

While his brother Julio Jr. found solace in sports, and his sister Chabeli launched a modeling career, Enrique found another outlet for his pent-up emotions. With no one to relate to except his nanny, brother, and sister, seven-year-old Enrique began to write down his thoughts in a journal. Whenever he was scared, or sad, or missing someone, Enrique would pour his feelings out onto the pages of his journal.

Eventually, his words became lyrics, and Enrique realized he wanted to be a singer. Even now, Enrique finds it hard to admit that he wanted to follow in his father's footsteps—after all, it was Julio's career that had helped to destroy his family. The need to be like his father—and to be nothing like his father—haunted Enrique.

By the time Enrique was fifteen, his journal was bursting with deeply personal songs. Still, he found it practically impossible to tell his parents about his singing ambitions. Enrique

was accustomed to expressing his innermost thoughts in writing. Talking about them was difficult.

One day while walking home from school, Enrique heard a beautiful melody drifting out of Little Havana, a popular local restaurant. Curious to see the source of the music, Enrique wandered in. Two local musicians, Mario Martinelli and Roberto Morales, were strumming guitars and singing. When their set ended, Enrique got up his nerve to approach their table and introduce himself. He was careful not to use his last name. He asked the men if they would help him compose songs. Impressed by his pluck and initiative, the musicians invited Enrique to sing for them after school one day.

While living in Miami, Enrique was exposed to a thriving music scene. Even as a teenager, he dazzled musicians Mario Martinelli and Roberto Morales with his powerful voice. With their help, Enrique was soon on his way to a successful singing career.

Enrique has always striven to make every performance unforgettable. And his devotion to his fans had been met with cheers and millions of record sales around the world.

With journal in hand, Enrique marched into Morales' basement fully prepared to impress the two musicians. It was the first time he had ever sung to an audience. Morales and Martinelli, unaware he was Julio Iglesias' son, were struck by Enrique's strong voice. For such a small, skinny kid, he sure could sing, they thought. They were more in awe when he revealed who his father was.

But Enrique had dazzled the musicians on his own, only revealing his last name *after* his performance. That gave him an inner strength and confidence that was apparent to those around him. His siblings even teased that he had a new girlfriend. Little did they know their brother had started an even more significant relationship – one with music.

Enrique spent every free moment with Martinelli and Morales. The two men became Enrique's vocal coaches and closest friends. Under their tutelage, Enrique's confidence and self-assurance grew. Still, he did not reveal the nature of his after-school activities. His family—his father!—had no idea what he was doing.

Eventually, Enrique realized that if he ever wanted to make it as a performer, he needed to come clean. He decided to involve someone who could take him to the next level, someone who was close to his family—and close to his father.

4

WHO'S
THAT BOY?

All through high school, Enrique continued to eat, sleep, and dream music. Instead of getting caught up in football, pep rallies, and girls, he spent hours locked in his room, composing lyrics or listening to his favorite artists – Fleetwood Mac, Dire Straits, Billy Joel, Journey, and John Mellencamp. Enrique's graduation in 1993 gave him a sense of closure, but it also signaled a new beginning for the budding musician.

Still afraid to tell his father about his musical aspirations, Enrique satisfied another ambition (and fulfilled his father's wish) by attending college. Music remained his top priority, however, and he didn't intend to let college get in the way. He told himself he'd work toward a degree in business administration, while he waited for his big breakthrough.

The University of Miami put other areas of Enrique's life on course. For the first time, he was dating, making friends, and gaining some much-needed independence. Enrique had always lived under his father's thumb, and now he was free to find his special place in the world.

Being on his own gave Enrique the clarity to see what

Enrique's good looks and style have won him fans in the music and fashion worlds.

he really wanted in life. Although he excelled in school, he never lost sight of his goal. He realized he was not cut out for the life of the nine-to-five businessman, and dropped out of college in his sophomore year. He saw a future for himself in show business.

"I packed my bags and left, and said, 'If it goes well, it goes well. If it goes wrong, I have no one to blame.'"

Only his closest friends knew of Enrique's departure from school. His parents went on believing that their youngest son was still hitting the books, and Enrique did nothing to dispel the myth. Keeping up the charade was easier than disappointing his family. If Enrique could land a recording contract and a best-selling record, his parents' happiness might overshadow his deceit.

Most importantly, Enrique wanted to make —or break—it on his own.

"It hurt me to keep a secret from my parents," he admitted. "But if I hadn't, I wouldn't be where I am now."

Enrique didn't head off on the road to fame without bringing help. He knew that his father's manager of the past nine years, Fernan Martinez, could help him succeed in the music industry. At first, the thought of confiding in someone so close to his father seemed a little crazy. But Enrique had grown close to Fernan and believed he could trust his old friend not to betray him.

Enrique asked the unsuspecting Fernan to meet with him, and once he settled in, Enrique launched into five well-rehearsed songs. He may have been performing for one man, but to Enrique, it seemed this moment would determine the rest of his life. It was imperative that his show be flawless.

And what of the performance? Did Fernan see greatness in front of him?

"It was beautiful," Fernan sighed. "The expression, the eyes, the hands, the body. You could see how much he believed in what he's singing."

Fernan was so impressed with Enrique's grace and skill that he agreed to foster and support Enrique's career. Fernan figured the younger Iglesias would have no problem landing a recording contract. Then Enrique made one important request: Fernan couldn't market Enrique as Julio's son. Eschewing his birthright, Enrique asked that Fernan not use his real last name. If Fernan truly wanted to help him, he would market Enrique Martinez.

Fernan couldn't understand why Enrique would want to make things more difficult for himself, but he relented. "Enrique Martinez" would succeed on his own merits and not on the merits of his famous last name.

Fernan sent out Enrique's demo record, using his alias, to the major labels, including Sony, EMI Latin, and PolyGram Latino. Every big recording house turned him down. They all had the same complaint: Enrique was too young, and people wouldn't like that kind of music coming from a young guy. At the time, Latin music was very conventional. Older singers ruled the charts. Here was this "young guy" singing Spanish ballads normally reserved for men three times his age!

The simplicity of his songs was another strike against Enrique. "Spanish record companies, they make music that is so complicated," Enrique complained, "with too

Once the little boy who locked himself in his bedroom, pouring his feelings into a beat-up journal, Enrique has taken his place at the forefront of the Latin music scene, recording hit albums for a world-wide audience.

many chords, too many changes, too many cheesy lyrics—instead of being direct and to the point."

Enrique had grown up listening to American music, and he preferred the simple melodies and meaningful lyrics. The songs on his demo were a seamless fusion of his Spanish and American roots, and while Enrique was broaching new multicultural territory, the record companies were stuck in the old school.

Just as he was about to give up, Enrique received news from a small label that specialized in Mexican music. Fonovisa Records liked what it heard, and signed Enrique Martinez to a three-album deal for a total of one million dollars. It wasn't the money or eminent fame that made Enrique happy. He was overjoyed that they'd chosen him for his music, not for being an Iglesias. The fact that Fonovisa had no idea that he was Julio's son gave Enrique a deep sense of satisfaction. He had accomplished something really big, by himself, on his own terms.

When Enrique signed the contract using his real name, Fonovisa executives were stunned. They couldn't believe that they had unknowingly signed the son of one of the biggest recording stars of all time! Perhaps to award Fonovisa for believing in his talent and not in his famous name, Enrique decided to let the company use his legal name to market his soon-to-be released record. Besides, he didn't want to kick off his career as an impostor. He was Enrique Iglesias, after all.

Enrique flew to Toronto, Canada, and began recording his self-titled debut album. He enjoyed the isolation of Canada. A change in scenery, he thought, was all he needed to ease the pressure and secrecy associated with Miami.

Now twenty, Enrique relied on the contents of his old journal for inspiration. He wanted his songs to be biographical, and his diary best represented what it felt like to be young and alone. He didn't just imagine pain, heartache, and loneliness; Enrique *lived* it.

"When I sing, mainly when I write a song, if I do not feel it," he confessed, "I do not write it."

Judging by the titles on his first album, Enrique felt a profound sense of abandonment as a child. Songs like "Si Tu Te Vas" (If You Leave), "Si Juras Regrasar" (If You Swear to Return), and "Falta Tanto Amor" (So Much Love Lost) recalled lost loves and broken promises. Enrique's mature lyrics belied his young years.

It took Enrique five months to complete the songs for his first album. Using his journal, dredging up old wounds, wrestling with demons, took a toll. Enrique found the songwriting process painful—but necessary. With the completion of each song, a little part of Enrique died, only to be replaced by the strength and confidence of the man he was fast becoming.

Enrique dedicated his debut album to someone who helped him through the pain of his youth, his beloved caretaker Elvira. "She gave part of her life to us. She filled the gap," he said.

When *Enrique Iglesias* was finally finished, Enrique selected "Si Tu Te Vas" as the first single. His record label sent the song out to a roster of radio stations, and before long, listeners everywhere were calling their local DJs and requesting the gorgeous ballad.

Amazingly, these fans still had no idea of the singer's true identity. Billed simply as "Enrique," Fonovisa wanted to measure the impact the song would have on listeners, without a famous last name complicating matters.

With the album's full release on September

Although millions would disagree, Enrique never saw himself as a star or heartthrob.

25, 1995, millions of people would discover the man behind the curtain. And his own father was among those about to make the discovery.

TO LIVE
HIS OWN LIFE

The release of *Enrique Iglesias* meant no more hiding for the young singer. Large posters featuring Enrique's face and full name hung in record stores and caused an immediate stir. It was impossible not to see the resemblance between father and son.

The album was so successful in the first few weeks of its release, that Enrique began to get offers for interviews, magazine covers, and television shows. He knew it wouldn't be long before his parents learned of his triumphant arrival on the music scene. The time had come to reveal his secret —and quickly.

Enrique chose a very public environment to break the news to his father. Figuring there would be safety in numbers, Enrique approached his father at a large party and told him everything. From leaving college to signing a recording contract to spending five months in Toronto, Enrique came clean.

At first, Julio stared in disbelief. He was torn between his displeasure at being kept in the dark and his elation over his son's desire to follow in his footsteps.

"My father and I spoke after he found out, and he was

After the successful English-language debuts of stars like Jennifer Lopez, Shakira, Marc Anthony, and Ricky Martin—Enrique's good looks, catchy rhythms, and charisma on stage made him a natural choice for the next crossover king.

shocked," remembers Enrique. "I said, 'Look, this is exactly what I've always wanted to do. Just let me do it my way, please.'"

Enrique's need to blaze his own trail, to do it his way, was soon tested. Upon hearing his son's secret, Julio wasted no time trying to advise Enrique on managing his career. After all, Julio had spent more than two decades learning the ins and outs of the music industry and could not wait to impart this wealth of knowledge to his son. The trouble was, Enrique no longer yearned for his father's guidance.

In an effort to keep control of his career, Enrique refused his father's counsel. It wasn't that he did not love Julio; he just didn't want to depend on him.

After coming clean with Julio, it was time to include his mother on all the changes in his life. Like Julio, Isabel was shocked to learn that her son was no longer a college man. Upon hearing that Enrique had traded books for a microphone, Isabel crossed herself and began praying for her son's future. She had lived through the terror of her father-in-law's kidnapping and had worried about the safety of her three children. She knew that her son's position in the limelight would be both a blessing and a curse.

Enrique could now enjoy his career with a clear conscience, and he had a lot to celebrate. On November 6, 1995, his single "*Si Tu Te Vas*" reached number six on the Latin *Billboard* charts. Within a few weeks, it soared to the number one position. Within days of its release, the second single, *"Experiencia Religiosa,"* made it to number three on the charts. His album also was flying up the charts, hovering at number three. This was phenomenal success for a newcomer!

To capitalize on his album's popularity, Enrique launched a massive publicity campaign. First, his publicity manager at Fonovisa booked him on countless radio and television shows. Next, Enrique toured record stores around the world. At one appearance in Los Angeles, three thousand screaming girls showed up to see the singer. The crowd was so huge, that security had to escort a flustered Enrique through the mob scene.

Eager to get close to the hot rising star, Enrique's fans clamor for autographs at his appearances.

More exposure came with Enrique's appearance on NBC's *Hard Copy*. After the show aired, millions of viewers began to flood Fonovisa with phone calls, some proposing marriage. Pounds of fan mail arrived daily.

As Enrique appeared more and more in the public eye, his famous father became a favorite topic of conversation for television interviewers. Once a reporter introduced Enrique simply as "the son of Julio Iglesias." Tired of the constant allusions to his father, as well as accusations of having depended on his father for vocal training and business management, Enrique strolled out of the TV studio, never looking back.

Enrique wanted to be seen as his own person, not as an extension of his father. But subduing the media's interest in the father/son comparison proved difficult. At the same time Enrique's new album was getting airplay, Julio released "*Balia Morena*," (Dance Baby) his first single off *his* new album, *La Carretera* (The Highway). The press had a field day setting up imaginary rivalries between Enrique and Julio —especially when Enrique's first single skyrocketed to number one while Julio's barely crawled to number twelve.

The harder the media tried to play one Iglesias off of the other, the more Enrique and Julio avoided talking about each other's careers. Of course, their refusal to discuss their private affairs just added fuel to another fire. The media began speculating that Enrique and Julio were getting ready to collaborate on a project.

"Is there any chance you and your father will record a duet anytime soon?" reporters asked Enrique.

Neither one had any interest in making music together. Julio thought Enrique had too much to learn about the industry. And Enrique wanted nothing more than to escape the clutches of his father.

Enrique had every reason to believe that he could succeed on his own terms. During the next year, *Enrique Iglesias* would sell more than five million copies, and plans for a world tour were set into motion.

But Enrique knew that it would take more than a best-selling debut album to secure his place in the music industry's upper echelon. He needed to release another album—one that was even better than his first. Enrique knew that the critics were just waiting for him to produce a flop, eager to see him land on his face in the much-feared sophomore slump. He wanted to prove to the critics, to the world, to himself, that he wasn't just a one-hit-wonder.

Deciding to stick with his winning formula of heartfelt ballads and Latin pop, Enrique focused on writing songs that were personal and intimate in nature. He had matured in the two years since *Enrique Iglesias*, and his new songs showed the wisdom and confidence of a true professional. "It took ten months to finish, and I am more satisfied with it," reported Enrique.

Vivir (To Live) surpassed all expectations—critics' and his own. Released on January 29, 1997, Enrique's second effort garnered rave reviews. Wrote one music critic: "You'll be hard-pressed to find a better new pop album than *Vivir*. Sung entirely in Spanish, it is filled with catchy, well-produced songs you'll find yourself humming after the first playing."

What's more, in it's first week out, *Vivir* sold

Along with singers like Ricky Martin, Marc Anthony, and Jennifer Lopez, Enrique led a revolution in Latin music, reaching new and enthusiastic audiences around the world.

five million copies throughout South and Central America, Europe, and Asia. Never before had a Latin artist sold so many albums in so little time! Enrique's winning streak didn't end there. Before long, *Vivir* went platinum in Taiwan, a victory no other Latin artist had ever achieved.

Enrique was unstoppable, outselling other Latin singers with amazing ease. Nobody could compete with his accomplishments—not even his father. Julio had released a new album, called *Tango*. He was shocked to learn that

Enrique's album was selling twice as fast as his own!

Enrique could barely stop long enough to enjoy all of his successes. Less than a month after the release of *Vivir*, Enrique received a Grammy nomination for Best Latin Pop Performance. Not only was this the ultimate in musical recognition, Enrique's nomination was for the same award that Julio had been up for the year before!

His family couldn't believe how far Enrique had come. It wasn't so long ago that they were teasing him about his journal writing—and now, with his Grammy nomination, they were showering him with admiration.

His brother Julio Jr. and sister Chabeli were confident that Enrique would walk away with a Grammy, but Enrique was not so sure. He was up against some pretty stiff competition, namely Luis Miguel, the odds-on favorite to win. As Enrique was about to find out, there are no guarantees in life—or in award shows.

6

LANGUAGE
OF THE HEART

February 26, 1997, was Grammy day. Enrique, like the rest of the nominees, awoke early and started getting ready for his big television appearance. The Grammys were being broadcast all over the world, and he knew that an expected 1.5 billion people would be watching.

While part of him was excited to be part of the pomp and circumstance, another part was strangely detached. Because Enrique was not favored to win, he approached the big day with calculated reserve. He had other priorities aside from winning a trophy, and he didn't want a possible Grammy clouding his vision. He was first and foremost a songwriter, whether he came home with a little gold gramophone or not.

"If they give the prize to me, I will feel very grateful, as I feel now about the nomination," he told a reporter from the Associated Press. "But if it does not happen, it will not change anything, since my greater challenge is to continue singing."

Try as he may to remain calm, cool, and collected, Enrique got caught up in the Grammy excitement. When he arrived at Los Angeles' Shrine Auditorium,

---

In 1997, Enrique's hard work and talent were rewarded with a Grammy award for his album *Vivir*. After dozens of appearances on talk shows and in record stores, this was Enrique's first time on a stage.

Enrique was surrounded by many of the musicians he had grown up listening to as a boy. Enrique was star struck. He couldn't believe that he was a part of all this incredible talent. It finally occurred to him that he was no longer an industry outsider. Enrique had made it!

He was having such a good time that he practically forgot why he was there. When the category for Best Latin Pop Performance was announced, he practically jumped out of his seat. All of a sudden, Enrique wanted to win—more than anything.

It seemed like an eternity before the presenter announced the winner. "And the Grammy goes to," he said, fumbling with the envelope, " . . . Enrique Iglesias!"

For a brief moment, Enrique thought he was hearing things. Could it be? Did they just call his name? He walked to the stage in a daze. At the podium, he looked out over a crowd of people who were applauding *just for him.* He composed himself as best he could, took a deep breath, and said, "Thank you."

Amazingly, this was the first time Enrique had been on stage. He had toured plenty of record stores, appeared on countless talk shows, sat in dozens of radio booths—but he had never actually stepped out on a stage. Winning a Grammy changed all that. Now, thousands of his fans wanted to see their favorite singer in concert. Enrique must heed their call.

Plans for a 13-country *Vivir* tour were set into motion. With more than sixty-seven concerts scheduled all over the world, Enrique set out to make every show unforgettable. He spared no expense. Whether it was set design, lighting, wardrobe, or sound, Enrique wanted everything to be perfect.

His efforts paid off. Shows in Mexico and Argentina—with arena capacities of 35,000 people—sold out in seconds! His fans could not get enough of him. Enrique's concerts were a mix of show-stopping effects (for one song, Enrique rode atop a crane, high over the audience), and intensely emotional singing. Sometimes he got so carried away by what he was singing, he stretched and pulled at his already torn T-shirt, causing female fans to scream with delight.

All this emotion was no stage act. "It's completely sincere," he said. "Not only the lyrics and the music, but the singer. It's real. I will never sing a song I don't feel. I will never write a song that doesn't have to do with me. That's something you can't fake. You can fool one person, but you can't fool ten million people."

Enrique's down-to-earth personality was just as sincere as his songwriting. Having grown up with the trappings of his father's celebrity, Enrique wasn't impressed by fancy cars and designer clothing. This jeans and T-shirt guy preferred McDonald's hamburgers to filet mignon and evenings in front of the television to velvet-roped nightclubs. He was so modest that when *People en Español* named him the Sexiest Man in the World, Enrique joked that his record label "bought" him the title.

As soon as Enrique wrapped up the *Vivir* tour, he marched right back into the studio and began recording his third album, *Cosas del Amor* (The Things of Love). Now a globe-trotting twenty-three-year-old, Enrique was eager to set his amazing experiences to music and decided to write six original songs for the album. To help with the remaining songwriting duties, Enrique enlisted the skills of Rafael Perez Botija, who had been such a vital part of *Vivir*. Enrique also cowrote a song, "*Dicen Por Ahí*" (They Say), with his old friend and mentor from Miami, Mario Martinelli.

The results were brilliant. But when the album hit the stores on September 22, 1998, the hot topic of conversation was not Enrique's songwriting abilities. Because of *Cosas del Amor*'s romantic lyrics, Enrique's love life became a popular subject of speculation. Surely his new album was dedicated to someone special.

The truth was, Enrique was writing about love, but his songs were about love lost, not gained. "Every time I write—I mean, I write about what's going on in my life," he revealed. "So there's got to be something—I mean, I've got to get dumped to write a good song."

The press was constantly trying to pair Enrique up with some beautiful Latina celebrity. For a while, rumors flew that he was dating Spanish model Estefanía Luyk. When word got out that he was seen strolling down the beach with former Miss Universe Alicia Machado, the gossip mushroomed out of control.

During one press conference, Enrique found himself being grilled on his romantic relationships. "I keep my private life private," Enrique responded, "and if I had one or have one, no one will know."

In reality, Enrique was far too busy to have a private life. His constant touring and endless hours in the recording studio left little room for

Enrique rings in the new millennium with a performance at radio station Z100's Jingle Ball.

romance. Enrique's life in the limelight also left little time for his family. His schedule was so crazy, he had to arrange appointments to call his mother.

The rest of the Iglesias clan also had full agendas. Julio Jr., following in his brother's footsteps, had launched a singing career and began modeling for Versace and Gap. Chabeli, proving show business was in her blood too, had inked a deal with US Spanish network television to host a talk show.

Enrique's time on the road also, ironically, brought him closer to his father. For the first time, Enrique understood the allure of performing in front of thousands of fans—and that gave him a deeper understanding of Julio. The need to perform was not just a passion, but an addiction. This awareness allowed Enrique to forgive Julio for his transgressions. The tension that Enrique had long experienced with his father was finally evaporating.

"A lot of people think me and my father don't get along," Enrique once told a reporter. "Of course we get along, and when it comes down to the real stuff, I'd kill for my father. I'm his number one fan. What my father has accomplished no one will ever accomplish. What I'm trying to accomplish now with Spanish music, he made easier and accomplished it twenty years ago and that's amazing."

As 1998 drew to a close, Enrique took stock on how far he had come—personally and professionally. No longer a lost little boy, the twenty-three-year-old had truly forgiven his father for his many disappointments and frustrations. Finally his own man, Enrique fully appreciated his own success.

By year's end, Enrique had sold thirteen million copies of his first three albums. His first tour in support of *Vivir* had spanned thirteen countries and made Enrique into a world-class entertainer. At the start of 1999, Enrique was ready to span the globe. It was time to conquer the United States.

7

ENRIQUE
GOES WEST

Enrique kicked off the U.S. leg of his *Cosas Del Amor* tour at the beginning of 1999. He knew that crossing over from the Latin to the North American market would be difficult, but 1999 was proving to be the year of the Latin invasion. English debuts of Jennifer Lopez, Shakira, Marc Anthony, and Ricky Martin were getting tons of airplay, and Enrique's good looks, catchy rhythms, and charismatic stage presence gave him a good shot at becoming the next crossover king.

McDonald's further guaranteed Enrique's firm American footing by sponsoring the U.S. leg of his tour. To show his gratitude, Enrique donated a portion of the concert proceeds to a scholarship program called the Hispanic American Commitment to Education Resources. Enrique became the program's official spokesperson and made his acting debut in a McDonald's Spanish-language commercial.

Enrique's next big opportunity came in the form of Will Smith. The actor/rapper had recently caught one of Enrique's electrifying performances and was so impressed by the singer's catchy grooves and overwhelming stage presence, he asked Enrique to contribute a song to the

Iglesias met Christina Aguilera when they sang a duet during the Super Bowl halftime show. Ever since, rumors of their romance have flourished.

After McDonald's helped sponsor Enrique's *Cosas Del Amor* tour, the singer donated a portion of the proceeds to a scholarship program called the Hispanic American Commitment to Education Resources and appeared in a McDonald's Spanish-language commercial.

soundtrack of his new movie, *Wild Wild West*.

Remembers Smith: "I went to one of Enrique's concerts and you've just never heard this kind of sustained screaming. . . . It was like the entire show. It was almost like people were coming there specifically to scream. And like the girls were taking turns going, 'Yeah!' And when [one girl's] getting ready to stop, she points to her girlfriend to take over . . . . I was like, I want this guy on the sound track."

Having strong ties to both his Latin and American background, Enrique was ready for the chance to record a song in English. Searching for something that would impress Will Smith, Enrique settled on "*Bailamos*"

(We Dance), a song that had been written several months before his U.S. tour. Now was the perfect time to pull the single out of storage.

The film's producers—and its star—were blown away by Enrique's song. They sent Enrique straight to the studio, where he pulled out all the stops. Appearing on a soundtrack was a great opportunity, and Enrique didn't want to take any chances.

To increase the song's buzz, Enrique shot two videos. One featured him as a gun-toting desperado, dancing with a flock of gorgeous young fillies. The second video followed Enrique as he romanced a sexy young lady.

"*Bailamos*" was released a couple of days after Will Smith's "*Wild Wild West*" single. From its first day out, it became one of the most requested singles in Miami and Los Angeles. Soon the whole country was dancing to Enrique's hot Latin pop.

With "*Bailamos*," Enrique joined the Latin craze that was sweeping the country. Radio stations across America couldn't keep Ricky Martin, Jennifer Lopez—and now Enrique Iglesias—off of their turntables. In a year where Latin music broke through to mainstream America, Enrique was among those leading the charge.

Just weeks after the record's release, Enrique landed squarely in the center of a major label bidding war. It was clear that he had huge crossover appeal, and executives from BMG, Warner Bros., and Universal/Interscope were courting Enrique with a vengeance. In the end, Enrique and his manager, Fernan Martinez, signed with Universal/Interscope, partly because the label supported

Enrique's desire to record his music in Spanish and English. The deal, worth $44 million, called for three albums in Spanish and three in English.

"Enrique has the power and charisma to move people," Jimmy Iovine, co-owner of Interscope said. "Every now and then, you find someone who is just very natural, who comes off like he owns it. It has nothing to do with the fact that he's a Latin artist. He's just a great artist."

Interscope wasted no time getting Enrique into the recording studio. The singer had to work extraordinarily hard to meet the album's tentative release date of November 1999. He wanted to top the success of his hot single "*Bailamos*," and he also had to complete the European leg of his *Cosas Del Amor* tour.

Enrique didn't let the pressure get to him. He delivered *Enrique*, an impeccably crafted album that would go on to sell five million copies around the world. A modern pop-meets-south-of-the-border fiesta, the album featured a duet with Whitney Houston, "Could I Have This Kiss Forever?" and a cover of Bruce Springsteen's "Sad Eyes." One critic raved about the record, calling Enrique's alluring voice, "rich and controlled, with appealing scratched-up edges and a masterful sense of musical balance."

Enrique wasn't without its share of controversies. In June of 2000, shock jock Howard Stern accused Enrique of not being able to sing. To defend himself, Enrique appeared on Stern's show and delivered a pitch-perfect rendition of "*Rhythm Divine*." In the end, Stern declared, "Wow. Well, you can sing."

Igesias's hit song "Bailamos" helped the soundtrack of Will Smith's film *Wild Wild West* reach double-platinum status.

Another distraction occurred later that year, when Enrique filmed the music video for the album's fourth single, "*Sad Eyes.*" The video, which is a cover of a Bruce Springsteen song, features Enrique in a see-through bath-tub with nineteen-year-old porn star Cassidey. Directed by edgy fashion photographer David LaChappelle, the video was deemed too steamy and suggestive for public viewing. MTV and VH1 refused to air it—and the video soon went down the drain.

These disputes hardly seemed to affect Enrique. In fact, he appeared to thrive on making things as difficult as possible for himself and then overcoming the obstacles. From his early days as Enrique Martinez to his latest foray producing the off-Broadway musical "4 Guys Name Jose," Enrique escaped his father's shadow and rose up to meet his success head on.

Determination and perseverance helped him achieve goal after goal. Yet, Enrique didn't want to be remembered for his multiple platinum albums or his award-winning performances. Enrique Iglesias just wanted the world to see him on very simple terms. Even though millions of women would disagree, Enrique didn't look at himself as a "star" or "heartthrob." When he looked at his reflection in the mirror, Enrique saw a performer—which was exactly what he set out to be.

All Enrique ever cared about was making music. In many ways, he was still the same little boy who locked himself in his bedroom, pouring his heart out into a beat-up journal. Even though he now could record in some of the most technologically advanced recording studios in the world, Enrique still found inspiration right in his own back yard.

"I need to be at home, sleeping there at least two weeks or even more and just writing in my room," he said. "That's where I write. Late at night in my room, when everyone is sleeping, from, like, two in the morning till eight o'clock in the morning."

It's a formula that continues to work for Enrique. In 2001, he was nominated for an American Music Award in the Favorite Artist Latin Music category. His single "*Be With You*"

garnered him a Grammy nomination in the Best Dance category. Currently working on his next Spanish-language album for Interscope, Enrique said he has never been happier.

"I'm in a privileged position right now, and just being able to do what I love is amazing," he said. "But if I'm married in ten years, I might just stay in the studio producing for other people. I'd like to do that at some point. But right now I want to go as far as I can as a performer." For Enrique, that may be a very long ride.

After releasing his first English-language album, *Enrique*, Iglesias performs the hit "Sad Eyes" at the GQ Men of the Year Awards.

CHRONOLOGY

1975   Enrique Iglesias Preysler born May 8, in Madrid, Spain

1979   Parents Isabel and Julio divorce

1982   Grandfather kidnapped and held for ransom

1990   Enrique begins singing and songwriting in private

1994   Gives private concert to Martinez

1995   Records first album, *Enrique Iglesias*

1996   Wins Grammy for Best Latin Pop Performer

1997   Records second album, *Vivir*

1998   Named *Billboard Magazine*'s Artist of the Year; judges first beauty pagent; records third album *Cosas Del Amor;* named *Billboard Magazine*'s Best Latin Pop Artist

1999   Serves as spokesperson for McDonald's HACER scholarship program; *Cosas Del* Amor tour sponsored by McDonald's; records single *Bailamos* for motion picture *Wild Wild West;* signs record deal worth $44 million with Universal/Interscope; records fourth record and first English-language album, *Enrique*

2000   Named *Billboard Magazine*'s Hot Latin Tracks artist of the year; appears on Howard Stern to defend his singing; produced off-Broadway show, "4 Guys"; Fonovisa releases *The Best Hits*"

ACCOMPLISHMENTS

Albums

1995	*Enrique Iglesias*
1997	*Vivir*
1998	*Cosas Del Amor*
1999	*Enrique* *Bailamos*
2000	*The Best Hits*

FURTHER READING

Granados, Christine. *Enrique Iglesias.* Delaware: Mitchell Lane Publishers, Inc., 2000.

Johns, Michael-Anne. *Enrique Iglesias.* Kansas City: Andrews McNeel Publishers, 2000.

Talmadge, Morgan. *Enrique Iglesias.* New York: Children's Press, 2000

INDEX

Photo Credits:

About the Author

This is CATHY ALTER ZYMET's fourth book. Her features, profiles, and short essays have appeared in the *Washington Post*, *Spin*, *Washingtonian*, *Preservation Magazine*, and the late, great *Might*. She lives in Washington, D.C., with her husband, Matt.